Dear Parents,

A love of reading is something we wish for every child. This book series is designed to encourage reading—with entry points appropriate to most any reader. Our well-defined levels help you choose books that are best suited to your child's interests and ability. These colorful books tap into a child's imagination and build confidence for a lifelong love of reading.

Our Read Smart bookmarks reinforce your child's reading vocabulary through games and activities. Take the time to make reading more fun by following the simple instructions on the bookmark.

Reading is a voyage that can take your child into wonderful, enchanting places. We are delighted to join you on this journey.

BEGINNING READER

For children who are ready to read their first books, know their letter sounds, and have developed an understanding of early phonics skills. Words include short vowels, simple plurals, and sight words.

DEVELOPING READER

For children who are ready for longer sentences and more lines of print per page. Stories are richer and include a growing vocabulary. Words feature beginning consonant blends.

CONFIDENT READER

For children who are ready for books with longer sentences and richer plots. Words are longer and feature ending consonant blends and simple suffixes.

ADVANCED READER

For children who are ready for books with more complex plots, varied sentence structure, and full paragraphs. Words feature long vowels and vowel combinations.

ISBN 1-60143-976-8

Hip-O
Wants to Play

Written by **Karen Baicker**
Illustrated by **Shawn Finley**

Hip-O wants to play.

Who will play with Hip-O?

Hip-O sees Pig Wig.

"Let's play tag," says Hip-O.

"Not now," says Pig Wig.

"I need to pack my bag!"

Who will play with Hip-O?

Hip-O sees Dog Bug.

"Let's race," says Hip-O.

"Not now," says Dog Bug.

"I need to nap."

Who will play with Hip-O?

Hip-O sees Pop Fox.

"Let's kick that can!"

"Not now!" says Pop Fox.

"I need this can!"

Hip-O sees the rats.

"Will you play a game?"

"Yes! Yes! We will play."

Hip-O yells, "This will be fun!"

But the rats see cheese.

Off run the rats!

Who will play with Hip-O?

Hip-O sits on a rock.

He is sad.

Pig Wig cannot play.

Dog Bug cannot play.

Pop Fox cannot play.

The rats cannot play.

Hip-O gets up to go.

But he falls in the mud!

Mud, mud, lots of mud!

What a mess!

Here comes Pig Wig!

She hops in the mud.

"Can I play?" says Dog Bug.

She hops in the mud too.

Pop Fox wants to play!

Here come the rats!

They all play in the mud.

What a mess! What fun!